T0132438

The Meanest Man on EARTH

To order additional copies of this book, contact:
Xlibris
1-888-795-4274
www.Xlibris.com
Orders@Xlibris.com

The
Meanest Man
on EARTH

Steve Dillon; Thomas Kalgreen

Many years ago, a blacksmith lived on the edges of a small and quaint village. He owned a wooden house that he had built by himself; outside he had an anvil, a hammer, and the other tools of his trade. There was a beautiful rose garden that was his pride and joy, and he had a rocking chair on his porch, which he used to rock himself to sleep after a hard day's work. He had built his house on the outskirts of the town because he liked to be alone, and most of the time the villagers let him be.

One year, when autumn was smiling down upon all the world with her brilliantly colored leaves, despite his desire to remain alone, the children of the village all of the sudden began coming to his home and running off with his tools, rocking in his chair, and picking roses from his garden.

This made the blacksmith mad, who yelled at the children and told them to leave him alone. He said that the children must be possessed by the Devil himself, and because of his attitude, the children called him the "meanest man on earth," even though he just wanted to be left alone.

Now, there was a beautiful good witch who was travelling through the town investigating the children's strange behaviors, and she heard all about this "meanest man on earth" from the disobedient children. After some thought, she decided to visit the blacksmith to determine if he really was as bad as the children had said (they were, after all, being influenced by the Devil himself!) To her surprise, when she visited the blacksmith, he made her a cup of tea, motioned for her to sit in his rocking chair, and offered her a bouquet of freshly cut roses. "He certainly isn't the meanest man on earth," she said to herself, and decided to grant the blacksmith three wishes.

The blacksmith was happy to have such magical power given to him, and he asked for the following three things: that if anyone were to pick up his hammer, it would shake the living daylights out of them until he told it to stop; that if anyone sat in his chair, it would rock the living daylights out of them until he told it to stop; and that if anyone were to pick a rose from his garden, the roses would envelop them and squeeze the living daylights out of them until he told them to stop. She kept up her end of the bargain and granted these wishes. Finishing her tea and going on her way, she waved to the blacksmith in farewell, promising that they would meet again.

Soon, the children of the village experienced the mystical enforcement of the blacksmith's ire and fled his home for their own after having the living daylights shaken, rocked, or squeezed out of them. They shouted even more that he was truly the meanest man on earth! Meanwhile, the Devil himself heard of the blacksmith through the children's claims that he was the meanest man on earth. The Devil said: "There is no way that this blacksmith can be meaner than I," and set about devising a plan to bring the blacksmith to where the Devil himself was to see just how mean he could be in the Devil's terrifying presence.

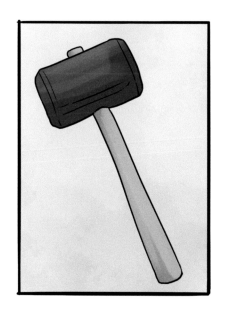  

The Devil told his youngest son, a little imp, to go bring the blacksmith to him. Upon reaching the blacksmith's home, the little devil said: "Blacksmith, you must come with me. My father wishes to see you." To this the blacksmith replied: "Of course... but I must finish these horseshoes first. Can you hand me my hammer so that I can finish and we'll be on our way?" The imp reached for the hammer and as soon as he grasped it, it began to shake him violently to and fro, so that he became frantic and cried out! The blacksmith allowed the hammer to shake the little devil a little more until the imp said: "Forget coming to see my father, just let me go!" So the meanest man on earth let the little devil go back to where he had come from.

When the Devil heard of this, he said to his oldest son: "You know what to do. Go bring me that blacksmith, and don't touch his hammer!" So the older devil approached the meanest man on earth and said: "You must come with me, my father wants to see you." Naturally, not wanting to go to where the Devil was at all, the meanest man on earth replied: "Go ahead and sit down on that rocking chair and rest; I must finish these horseshoes first." So the young devil sat down and he became stuck! The chair began to rock him violently to and fro, and the young devil grew sick. "Please let me go!" he eventually cried, and the blacksmith said: "If your father wants to see me so badly, tell him to come get me himself!"

So, back where they came from, the devils grumbled at their lack of success. The Devil himself replied: "I will go and bring this so called 'meanest man on earth' to me so that I can show him that I and only I am the true meanest man on earth!" When he arrived with a puff of smoke and a whiff of brimstone, he headed immediately to the outskirts of town where the blacksmith lived. Approaching him carefully and avoiding the hammer and the rocking chair, the Devil said: "You must come with me. I will prove to you once and for all that I am much meaner than you are!" To this the meanest man on earth replied: "Of course, but first would you help me pick some roses? I need to get this gardening done soon, before it rains."

The Devil saw no problem with this and said: "Certainly, sir, but then we must immediately go back to where I came from," and began to pick roses. As soon as the Devil touched the roses, however, the vines grew and squeezed him like a huge boa constrictor. He cried out: "Oh no! Let me go!" But the meanest man on earth said: "Only if you set the children of the village free!" The Devil replied: "Okay... just let me go!" The meanest man on earth released The Devil, and immediately the children of the village began to behave properly and obey their parents again.

The Devil went back to where he came from, and decided that from that day forward the blacksmith could be known as the meanest man on earth for all he cared, and that he would be left alone by the Devil's minions. On earth, outside the village, a butterfly transformed into the good witch, and she went to see the blacksmith, who had by this time changed his attitude and welcomed the children of the village to his home, where they were allowed to pick roses and sit in the rocking chair without having the living daylights shaken out of them. They were now obedient to their parents since being set free, and the blacksmith had no more reason to scold them. The good witch praised the blacksmith for his success in defeating the Devil and his minions, and granted him one more wish. After all was said and done, he wished for children of his own, and he and the good witch became engaged to get married!!!

Printed in the United States
By Bookmasters